Magic Betsey

D0626193

Also by Malorie Blackman

The NOUGHTS & CROSSES sequence:
NOUGHTS & CROSSES
KNIFE EDGE
CHECKMATE
DOUBLE CROSS

NOBLE CONFLICT

BOYS DON'T CRY

THE STUFF OF NIGHTMARES
TRUST ME
PIG-HEART BOY
HACKER
A.N.T.I.D.O.T.E.
THIEF!
DANGEROUS REALITY
THE DEADLY DARE MYSTERIES
DEAD GORGEOUS
UNHEARD VOICES
(A collection of short stories and poems, collected by Malorie Blackman)

For younger readers:
CLOUD BUSTING
OPERATION GADGETMAN!
WHIZZIWIG and WHIZZIWIG RETURNS
GIRL WONDER AND THE TERRIFIC TWINS
GIRL WONDER'S WINTER ADVENTURES
GIRL WONDER TO THE RESCUE

BETSEY BIGGALOW IS HERE!
BETSEY BIGGALOW THE DETECTIVE
BETSEY'S BIRTHDAY SURPRISE
HURRICANE BETSEY

For beginner readers:
JACK SWEETTOOTH
SNOW DOG
SPACE RACE
THE MONSTER CRISP-GUZZLER

Malorie Blackman

Illustrated by Jamie Smith

RED FOX

MAGIC BETSEY
A RED FOX BOOK 978 1 782 95187 2

First published in Great Britain in 1994 by Piccadilly Press Ltd

This edition published by Red Fox,
an imprint of Random House Children's Publishers UK
A Random House Group Company

This Red Fox edition published 2014

1 3 5 7 9 10 8 6 4 2

Text copyright © Oneta Malorie Blackman, 1994
Illustrations copyright © Jamie Smith, 2014

The right of Malorie Blackman to be identified as the author of this work has been asserted in accordance with the Copyright, Designs and Patents Act 1988.

All rights reserved. No part of this publication may be reproduced, stored in a retrieval system, or transmitted in any form or by any means, electronic, mechanical, photocopying, recording or otherwise, without the prior permission of the publishers.

The Random House Group Limited supports the Forest Stewardship Council® (FSC®), the leading international forest-certification organisation. Our books carrying the FSC label are printed on FSC®-certified paper. FSC is the only forest-certification scheme supported by the leading environmental organisations, including Greenpeace. Our paper procurement policy can be found at www.randomhouse.co.uk/environment.

Set in Bembo MT

RANDOM HOUSE CHILDREN'S PUBLISHERS UK
61–63 Uxbridge Road, London W5 5SA

www.**randomhousechildrens**.co.uk
www.**totallyrandombooks**.co.uk
www.**randomhouse**.co.uk

Addresses for companies within The Random House Group Limited can be found at: www.randomhouse.co.uk/offices.htm

THE RANDOM HOUSE GROUP Limited Reg. No. 954009

A CIP catalogue record for this book is available from the British Library.

Printed and bound in Great Britain by CPI Group (UK) Ltd, Croydon CR0 4YY

For Neil and Lizzy,
with love as always.

EAST SUSSEX SCHOOLS LIBRARY SERVICE	
567304	
Askews & Holts	Sep-2014
JF	£5.99

WITHDRAWN
EAST SUSSEX COUNTY COUNCIL

Malorie Blackman has written over sixty books and is acknowledged as one of today's most imaginative and convincing writers for young readers. She has been awarded numerous prizes for her work, including the Red House Children's Book Award and the Fantastic Fiction Award. Malorie has also been shortlisted for the Carnegie Medal. In 2005 she was honoured with the Eleanor Farjeon Award in recognition of her contribution to children's books, and in 2008 she received an OBE for her services to children's literature. She has been described by *The Times* as 'a national treasure'. Malorie Blackman is the Children's Laureate 2013–15.

Contents

Betsey and the Secret Weapon

"Go, Betsey! Go!"

Betsey ran as fast as she could – but it wasn't fast enough. Her best friend May flashed past her on the right. Josh whizzed by her on the left.

"Run, Betsey!"

Betsey could hear her bigger brother Desmond shouting to her. She tried to run faster but Josh and May and Ce-Ce were now way out in front. Betsey slowed down. She'd never catch them now.

"BETSEY, RUN!" Desmond yelled.

Betsey didn't stop but she didn't run

flat out either. What was the point? She'd never catch up with her friends now.

Betsey finished the race last. Desmond walked over to her and put his arm around her shoulders.

"Never mind, Betsey. You'll do better next time."

"No I won't," Betsey sniffed. "I'm a useless runner. Everyone always beats me. I bet even Gran'ma Liz could beat me!"

"I don't think so!" Desmond smiled.

"Yes, she could," Betsey insisted.

"It was only a practice run," Desmond pointed out. "The real race isn't until next

Friday. That gives you plenty of time to get better."

"I'm not going to run any more stupid races." Betsey kicked at the sand, her head bent.

May jogged over, puffing as she ran.

"Bad luck, Betsey. Better luck next time." May smiled.

"May, don't be such a show-off!" Betsey fumed. And off she marched.

"There's no need to bite my head off just because you lost!" May called after her. "Bad loser!"

Betsey ignored her and carried on

walking home. She'd never, ever won a race. Her friends always beat her and she always came last or close to it. She'd never be able to run. Never. Never. Never!

Desmond ran up and started walking beside her.

"Betsey, just do your best. That's all that matters," said Desmond.

"Botheration, Desmond, I *am* doing my best, but it doesn't get me anywhere – except last," sniffed Betsey.

"It's only a race," said Desmond.

"That's all right for you to say. You've never come last in a running race," said Betsey miserably.

Desmond chewed on his bottom lip and thought for a while.

"Betsey, if I tell you a secret, do you promise never to tell anyone else?" Desmond said at last.

Betsey stopped walking and looked up at her brother. He looked absolutely serious.

"I promise," Betsey breathed.

It wasn't often that Desmond shared his secrets!

"I always used to come last in my races," Desmond began. "Until something strange, something really *peculiar* happened."

"What was that?" Betsey asked.

Desmond looked around, first this way, then that, before he spoke.

"I found a secret weapon to help me with my running," Desmond whispered.

"A secret weapon? What was it?" asked Betsey, her eyes as round as saucers.

Desmond looked around again.

"A pair of running shoes," whispered Desmond.

"Is that all?" Betsey's shoulders slumped with disappointment.

"Ah, but they weren't just any old pair of running shoes. They were special. They were *magic*!"

"They were?"

Desmond nodded. "Every time I wore those shoes I never lost a race."

"Where are those shoes now?" Betsey asked.

"In a secret place." Desmond winked.

"Oh, Desmond, let me borrow them. Please!" Betsey begged.

Desmond studied Betsey closely. "Only

on one condition . . ." he said at last.

"Anything," Betsey interrupted.

She would agree to anything if it meant she could borrow Desmond's secret weapon.

"You can't tell anyone about them," said Desmond. "It's got to be our secret or the magic might not work."

"Agreed!" Betsey said at once.

"There's something else," said Desmond. He pulled Betsey closer.

"What's that?" Betsey asked.

"I'll give you the shoes tonight, but you've got to practise running and

running in them to get used to them. Then the shoes will know that they've got to transfer their magic from me to you," Desmond explained.

"I can do that," said Betsey. "I'll run in them every day until the race."

"D'you promise?" said Desmond.

"I promise," said Betsey.

She was going to use Desmond's secret weapon. She'd never lose another running race again!

Every day after that, Betsey wore Desmond's secret trainers. From the moment she put them on, they fitted perfectly. She even wanted to sleep in them but Gran'ma Liz put her foot down and wouldn't allow it.

And every day Betsey ran!

She ran before school and during the break times at school and after school. She ran everywhere, all day, every day until Gran'ma Liz said, "Betsey, if you're not careful, you'll run until there's nothing left of you but a greasy spot!"

Betsey didn't care. She carried on running.

At last Friday arrived – the school's sports day. It seemed like everyone in the district turned up. And Betsey's race was the next event. Betsey stood at the starting line with her other friends. But this time, she wasn't worried. Oh no! This time she had Desmond's secret weapon.

She was wearing his magic running shoes. They didn't look like much of a secret weapon. They were old and the bits that should have been white were now grey. But that didn't matter. Betsey could feel their magic spinning up through her legs right to the top of her head.

Desmond came running over.

"Ready, Betsey?" Desmond winked.

"Ready!" Betsey smiled.

"Remember, you've got to really believe in their magic and run flat out. Run harder than you ever have before and *don't give up*," said Desmond.

"OK." Betsey nodded.

She bent down and touched her secret weapons for luck.

Desmond ran back to the sidelines. Betsey waved at her whole family who had come to cheer her on. There was Mum, Gran'ma Liz and her bigger sister,

Sherena, as well as Desmond. Betsey sighed. It would've been wonderful if Dad could've been there as well, but he wasn't due home for another three weeks.

Betsey turned and looked down the beach to the finish line. She ignored the lapping of the sea on the sand. She ignored the birds singing in the coconut trees. She concentrated on the finishing line down the beach and nothing else.

"Are you all ready?" the judge called

out. "On your marks . . . GO!"

Betsey raced like the wind. She didn't look to see where anyone else was. She didn't pause or slow down but she kept her eyes on the finishing line. And in no time at all she was running past it.

"Hooray! Hooray! Well done, Betsey."

Betsey looked around. Mum and Sherena and Desmond were running up to her, followed by Gran'ma Liz.

"Did I win? Did I win?" asked Betsey.

She wasn't sure. "No. May came first – but you came second!" Sherena grinned.

Mum hugged Betsey tight. "I'm so proud of you, Betsey. Well done!"

Second . . .

"I didn't come first . . . but second is a lot better than coming last all the time!" Betsey decided.

Betsey ran over to her friend, May.

"Well done, May!" said Betsey.

"Congratulations, Betsey," said May. "You almost caught me. I only just won!"

"Maybe next time I'll beat you," said Betsey.

"Maybe . . . and maybe not!" said May.

Betsey laughed and ran back to her family. But then disaster struck! The sole of one of the trainers came unstuck and started flapping around under Betsey's foot like a bird's wing.

"Desmond, look! Look at your secret weapon," Betsey wailed. "How will I ever win another race now?"

"Betsey . . . I've got a confession to make," Desmond began. "Those running shoes . . . they're not really a secret weapon. They're not really magic."

"Yes, they are." Betsey frowned. "I wouldn't have come second if it wasn't for them."

"That was *you*, Betsey, not the shoes. They're just my old running shoes. You came second because you practised and you didn't give up," said Desmond.

Betsey looked down at the trainers. They didn't look so magic any more.

They just looked old and battered.

"They're not really magic . . . ?" Betsey asked.

Desmond shook his head.

Betsey slowly smiled. "Well, if they're not magic, then it must be *me*. I'm the secret weapon!"

"Too right!" Desmond grinned.

"I'm going to keep practising and I'm going to get better and better at running," Betsey smiled. "And, to be honest, Desmond, I'm glad these old running shoes aren't magic."

"Why?" asked Desmond.

"Because that means I can go back to wearing my own trainers again. I don't have to wear your ones any more," Betsey said. "Your trainers stink of pong-smelly cheese and there's nothing magic about that!"

Betsey and the Birthday Present

"Mum! Gran'ma Liz!" Betsey burst into the house and raced into the kitchen.

"Guess what? Guess what?" Betsey danced around the table.

"Go on then – as you're bursting to tell us!"

"It's May's birthday on Saturday and she's having a birthday party. I can go, can't I?" Betsey was so excited, she bounced up and down like a tennis ball.

"A party!" said Mum. "That'll be fun. Of course you can go, Betsey."

"Yippee! A party!"

Abruptly, Betsey stopped dancing. She turned quickly to her mum.

"Can I have a new dress, Mum? And new shoes to go with it? Can I? And a present for May?"

"Betsey, I'm not made of money!" Mum frowned.

"And money doesn't grow on trees," sniffed Gran'ma Liz.

"Yes it does," Betsey replied at once.

"Pardon?"

"Money is made of paper and paper comes from trees, so money *does* grow on trees," said Betsey. "We did paper at school!"

Mum and Gran'ma Liz looked at each other. Sherena burst out laughing.

"I'll tell you what, Betsey," said Sherena. "When you get some money, go and plant it, then wait for a money tree to grow! But make sure you tell me where you planted the money first!"

"Botheration, Sherena! You're just jealous because I'm going to a party on Saturday and you're not!" said Betsey. She turned to her mum and Gran'ma Liz. "When can we buy my new dress and my new shoes and a present for May?"

"As your mum's working, I'll take you shopping tomorrow after school," said Gran'ma Liz. "But you can't have all those things."

"But I want them," said Betsey. "I *need* them!"

"You could always *not* go to May's party," Gran'ma Liz pointed out.

Betsey opened her mouth to argue, then snapped it shut. She *was* going to May's party and she'd get a new outfit and a present for May if it was the last thing she did!

The following afternoon, Gran'ma Liz and Betsey headed off to the shops.

"Let's try this store," said Gran'ma Liz.

They walked in and passed the costume jewellery counter.

"Look!" Betsey tugged at Gran'ma Liz's arm, then pointed.

It was the perfect present. A silver-coloured bracelet with purple stones.

Gran'ma Liz looked at the price tag on the bracelet. "Hhmm! It's not exactly cheap!" she sniffed.

"But May would love it. Can we get my dress first and then come back?" asked Betsey.

They went to the children's section of the store and walked up and down, up and down the aisles.

"How about this dress?" asked Gran'ma Liz.

"Nah! Too boring!" Betsey replied.

"What about this one?" Gran'ma Liz asked.

"Nah! Too long!" said Betsey.

"What's wrong with this one?"

"Too horrible!"

Twenty minutes later, Gran'ma Liz was getting very fed up!

"Betsey, child! My feet are beginning to hurt," Gran'ma Liz said.

And then Betsey saw it! It wasn't a dress. It was a blouse – the exact same colour of the sea on a sunny day, with tiny white buttons. And it was beautiful.

"Can I have that blouse, Gran'ma Liz? It'd look excellent with my white skirt," said Betsey.

Gran'ma Liz looked at the price tag. She shook her head. "Betsey, this blouse is too expensive."

"But I *need* it," Betsey protested.

"Betsey, if we buy this blouse, there'll barely be enough money left over to buy May an ice-cream, let alone the bracelet!" said Gran'ma Liz firmly.

"But . . . but . . ." Betsey protested.

"You can have the bracelet for May *or* the blouse for yourself. I don't have enough money to buy both," Gran'ma Liz said. "Which one do you want? But just remember it's May's birthday – not yours."

Botheration! Betsey stared at the blouse. She wanted the blouse something fierce. The only trouble was – she wanted the bracelet too! Which one should she choose? She looked across the shop to the costume jewellery counter, then back at the blouse. Gran'ma Liz watched without saying a word.

"I'll . . . I'll have the blouse," Betsey said at last.

"Are you sure?" said Gran'ma Liz.

Betsey nodded. But inside, she didn't feel too sure at all . . .

All the way home on the bus, Betsey

held on to the carrier bag that had her blouse in it. She kept opening up the bag to look at it. It was so pretty. Betsey didn't even mind that she didn't get new shoes. She'd wear her sandals and *still* look good.

"But what about a present for May . . . ?" said a tiny voice inside Betsey. "What about May's birthday . . . ?"

"You're very quiet," said Gran'ma Liz as they got off the bus.

"Gran'ma, do you think I should have bought the bracelet for May instead of the blouse?" Betsey asked.

Gran'ma stroked Betsey's cheek. "Betsey, it was your decision. What do *you* think you should have done?"

"I don't know," Betsey replied.

"Then you'll have to work it out for yourself." Gran'ma Liz shrugged.

And they began to walk home, past the

sugar cane fields, past their neighbours' houses with their shady porches. One person waved at them, but Betsey was too busy thinking to notice.

Later that night, Betsey lay on her side in bed looking at the blouse she'd bought. The sea-blue blouse with white buttons. But the strange thing was, it didn't look as pretty as it did in the shop.

"What about a present for May . . . ?" The voice inside Betsey's head wouldn't leave her alone. It roared like the sea in a September storm. "A present for May . . . a present for May . . ." it said.

Betsey put her hands over her ears and turned her back on the blouse. All at once, she didn't even want to look at it any more.

On Thursday Betsey was very quiet and on Friday morning she was quieter still.

"Betsey dear, don't you feel well?" asked Gran'ma Liz.

Betsey shook her head slowly.

"What's the matter, child?" asked Gran'ma Liz.

"I hate that blouse. I hate it! I wish you'd never bought it," said Betsey.

"You liked it on Wednesday afternoon," Gran'ma Liz reminded her.

"Well, I don't like it now," said Betsey.

"Do you want me to take it back to the store?" asked Gran'ma Liz.

"Could you? *Would you*?" Betsey asked, hopefully.

"Do you want another blouse instead?" Gran'ma Liz asked.

Betsey shook her head. "Can you buy that bracelet we saw? The bracelet for May's birthday."

Gran'ma Liz smiled. "Are you sure?"

Betsey nodded.

"Then I'll go and exchange the blouse

today, while you're in school," said Gran'ma Liz.

Betsey skipped out of the room. All at once, she felt a whole lot better.

The next day at May's party, Betsey handed over her present which was now wrapped up. May tore off the wrapping paper and squeaked with delight when she saw the bracelet.

"Oh Betsey, thank you. It's beautiful," breathed May. "I'll wear it every day."

"You look pretty, Betsey," said Ce-Ce. "I like your top."

Betsey looked down at her yellow blouse and her white skirt. She smiled at Gran'ma Liz, then turned to Ce-Ce and said, "It's not new. I've had this blouse for ages."

"But you still look pretty," smiled Gran'ma Liz. "You've never looked prettier."

"Look, everyone! Look at what Betsey bought me!" May called out.

And Betsey joined the others who were all around May, admiring her new bracelet.

Get Lost, Betsey!

Betsey hopped from foot to foot as if her toes were on fire. Today was going to be an excellent day! Betsey and her family were all going to the market – and oh, how Betsey loved the market! But there was an extra special reason why Betsey was so excited.

"Dad's coming home soon!" Betsey beamed.

"Not until next week, Betsey," Sherena reminded her.

"But next week is sooner rather than later," Betsey pointed out.

Dad was abroad studying to be a doctor and it'd been ages since Betsey had last seen him. Although he sent lots of emails and Skyped almost every other day, it just wasn't the same.

But at last he was coming home.

That's why Betsey's whole family were going to market, to get in all of Dad's favourite foods and to buy other things to make him feel really welcome.

"Hurry up, Sherena. You're too slow! If we wait for you, we'll never get to town."

Betsey ran over to Sherena and started tugging up the zip at the back of her dress.

"OUCH!" Sherena yelled. "Betsey, you're supposed to zip up the dress, not my skin!"

"I'm only trying to help," said Betsey.

"Then get lost and leave me to do it," said Sherena. "Your kind of help is too painful!"

Betsey raced into Desmond's room.

"Desmond! You're not ready. Hurry up!" said Betsey.

"I just need to put my shoes on," said Desmond.

"I'll get them for you," Betsey offered.

Betsey saw Desmond's shoes under his bed and ran past him to get them.

"OW! Betsey, those are my toes, not the carpet," Desmond yelled as Betsey trod on his foot!

"It's OK, you've got five more!" said

Betsey, pointing to the foot she *hadn't* stepped on.

"That's not funny!" fumed Desmond.

"Don't be such a grouchy potato head!" said Betsey.

"I'll stop being a grouch if you go away, get lost, close the door on your way out, put an egg in your shoe and beat it, make like a tree and leave!" Desmond said.

"All right! I'll go. But I don't care what you say to me today, because we're going into town. *And Dad's coming home soon!*" Betsey smiled.

Betsey darted out of the room.

SMACK! She crashed straight into

Sherena. And was Sherena pleased? No, she wasn't.

"Betsey, why don't you watch where you're going?" snapped Sherena.

"She's a real pest, isn't she?" Desmond agreed.

"That's quite enough from both of you." Gran'ma Liz appeared from nowhere and glared at Sherena and Desmond. "You two say sorry to your sister."

"Sorry, Betsey," Sherena and Desmond said at once.

They'd both seen that look on Gran'ma Liz's face before and they weren't about to argue!

“Now let’s get going!” Gran’ma Liz smiled.

And at last they were off.

When they got off the bus in town, Betsey hardly knew where to look first. All different kinds of fish and flowers and food and fruit filled the market stalls. Paw-paws, mangoes, bananas, cherries, sugar apples and coconuts on some stalls. Swordfish, flying fish, red mullet and salt fish on others. Sweet potatoes, yams, breadfruits, green bananas, eddoes and okras on still more. Betsey didn't even want to blink, in case she missed something.

"Gran'ma Liz! Isn't it extra-amazing?" asked Betsey, her eyes wider than wide.

"Yes, child," smiled Gran'ma Liz. "And tiring! And noisy!"

Betsey and her family weaved their way through the masses of people, looking at stall after stall.

“Betsey, stay close to me. I don’t want you wandering off,” said Gran’ma Liz.

“No, Gran’ma.”

“Mum, I’m just going to do some window shopping,” said Sherena.

“I think I’ll join you,” said Desmond.

“Can I come? Let me come!” said Betsey.

“No way!” Desmond and Sherena said at once.

Gran'ma Liz looked at Sherena and Desmond. "You two aren't being very kind to your sister today. Betsey, go along with them, but don't give them any trouble."

Betsey grinned up at Desmond and Sherena. She was happy about going with them, even if they weren't!

"I'll meet you three at Joe's ice-cream stand in an hour," said Mum, glancing down at her watch.

"Come on then, Betsey," tutted Sherena.

And off Desmond and Sherena marched. Betsey had to trot to keep up with them but she didn't mind. It was better than being with the grown-ups!

"Keep up with us, Betsey," said Desmond. "We don't want you slowing us down."

"Don't worry," said Betsey.

On the very next stall there were coconut cakes, all kinds of doughnuts, fresh biscuits and her favourite – banana fritters! They all smelt so scrumptious. Betsey stopped and breathed deeply to get the full effect.

"Look at these!" Betsey called out to her brother and sister who were now some way ahead of her.

"Betsey, get a move on," Sherena called back before she carried on walking.

Betsey ran to catch up with them – and then she saw it! A toy stall! There were rows and rows of dolls, magic playing cards, board games, bouncing balls and . . . *marbles*. Betsey had never seen so many marbles. Hundreds and hundreds of them piled up in buckets. Big ones, little ones, bright ones, glittering ones, marbles that were all one colour and marbles where all the colours fought for space to shine.

"D'you like my marbles?" The woman on the stall smiled.

"Oh yes!" breathed Betsey. "They're beautiful."

"Bring your mum along and I'll sell you some," said the woman.

Mum! Betsey looked around quickly. Where were Sherena and Desmond? Where were Mum and Gran'ma Liz? She couldn't see any of them.

Betsey jumped up and down, trying to see over the heads of all the grown-ups around her, but they were too tall. Betsey's heart suddenly began to hammer in her chest. She raced forward, looking for Desmond and Sherena.

They were nowhere to be found. Betsey ran past stall after stall but . . . nothing. She turned around but she didn't see anything or anyone she recognised.

"Botheration!" said Betsey. She said it two more times! "Botheration! Botheration!"

"I'll go back and try to find Mum and Gran'ma Liz," Betsey decided.

Betsey headed back the way she'd just come but that didn't do any good either. There was noise and bustle and fuss everywhere Betsey turned. The market wasn't a wonderful place any more. It was big and noisy and frightening. Betsey began to sniff. Her eyes started to sting with tears.

"If you cry, you won't see anything at

all," Betsey muttered sternly to herself.

But it didn't help.

All Betsey wanted to do now was find Mum and go home.

"Hello, sugar. Did you find your Mum? Are you going to buy some of my marbles?"

Betsey turned her head. She was in front of the toy stall again. The woman behind the stall smiled at Betsey – and that was it. Betsey burst into tears!

'What's the matter?" Immediately the woman came out from behind her stall and squatted down in front of Betsey. "Are you all right?"

"I can't find my mum." Betsey wiped her eyes.

"Hhmm!" said the woman. "I think

the best thing to do is find a policeman. D'you agree?"

Betsey nodded. The stall woman stood up and looked around.

"There's one. OFFICER!"

A policeman came over to the toy stall.

"What's the problem?" asked the policeman, smiling kindly at Betsey.

"I can't find my mum," said Betsey.

"Where d'you live?" asked the policeman.

Betsey had just opened her mouth to tell him, when, "BETSEY!"

And Betsey was swept off her feet and hugged so tightly by her mum that she could hardly breathe. Betsey looked around. Sherena, Desmond and Gran'ma Liz were all trying to hug her too!

"Elizabeth Ruby Biggalow! You had us all worried sick," said Gran'ma Liz.

"I know this morning, we told you to get lost . . ." began Sherena.

"But we didn't mean it," finished Desmond.

"Sherena and Desmond, the next time you take your sister somewhere with you, don't wander off and leave her to get lost," said Mum firmly.

"I wasn't lost. I knew exactly where I was," said Betsey. "I was in the market, looking for all of you. That means you were the ones who were lost, not me!"

"Betsey!" Sherena shook her head as everyone else laughed. "I wonder about you sometimes. I really do!"

Magic Betsey!

"Ladies and gentlemen, Betsey the Great, Betsey the Wonderful, Betsey the Magnificent will now put on a magic show for you! A magic show so excellent that nothing like it has ever been seen before and will never be seen again."

"Betsey, get on with it," Desmond said.

Betsey ignored him! She wasn't Betsey Biggalow, Desmond's sister any more. Oh no! She was Betsey the Magician! Betsey's Uncle George had bought her a book on magic tricks and Betsey had spent the last few days reading it and practising her tricks over and over. And now she was ready.

Betsey looked down at the table which had all the things she needed for her magic tricks on it.

"What shall I do first?" Betsey wondered out loud.

"Today, Betsey! Today!" said Sherena. "I've got other things to do, you know."

"Botheration, Sherena. You can't rush real magic!" Betsey said. Being a magician was hard work!

"Mum, can I leave?" Sherena asked.

"No!" Mum said firmly. And that was the end of that!

"OK then," said Betsey. "Before I do anything else, I have to wave my magic wand over this table or none of my tricks will work."

Betsey picked up her wand. She'd made it by covering the ends of a twig from the garden with some tinfoil and it looked perfect! She waved it over the table and said the magic words, "Betsey Magic! Magic Betsey! Do your magic! Show us! Let's see!"

"Oh, good grief!" said Desmond.

Gran'ma Liz gave him one of her looks and he shut up!

"For my first trick, I'm going to ask Sherena to pick a card," said Betsey.

She walked over to Sherena and fanned all the cards out in front of her, face down.

"Pick a card then," Betsey urged.

Sherena picked out a card and looked at it.

"Now put it back," said Betsey.

Carefully, Sherena put the card back into the middle of the pile. Betsey split the pile of cards into two and turned to walk back to the table. She knew Sherena's card was the one on top of the pile in her left hand. She picked it up and stuffed it up her shirt sleeve, keeping it in place by squeezing her arm against her side. It was difficult – especially as her sleeves were short! Then Betsey turned around to face her audience.

"I will now shuffle the cards and produce Sherena's card by magic!" said Betsey.

"And some cheating while your back

was turned," muttered Desmond.

"I don't need to cheat. I'm a real magician," Betsey said loftily. She shuffled the cards, tapped them with her wand, then shuffled them again. But this time she quickly tried to reach up and fish the card out of her sleeve at the same time. It didn't work. The cards flew out of her hands and up into the air.

"BETSEY! Those are my cards you're bending and ruining," said Sherena.

"Botheration, Sherena. I'm not ruining your cards. They're ruining my trick!" said Betsey.

Mum and Gran'ma just looked at each other. Betsey bent down to pick up the cards that now lay scattered at her feet.

RIP! As Betsey tugged at the card beneath her left foot, half of it stayed under her foot and the other half was left in Betsey's hand.

"Betsey! I told you to be careful with my cards." Sherena sprang off the sofa. "Look what you've done!"

"Sorry, Sherena. It wasn't deliberate," Betsey said quickly.

"Is that it then?" asked Desmond, standing up. "Can we go now?"

"But I haven't finished," said Betsey.

Desmond sat down again. They all waited for Betsey to move on to her next trick.

"This next one is a water trick," said Betsey. "But first I have to say the magic words – 'Betsey Magic! Magic Betsey! Do your magic! Show us! Let's see!'"

Betsey picked up a glass off the table.

"I'm holding an ordinary glass of water in my right hand and an ordinary piece of card in my left hand," said Betsey.

She walked over to Mum. "I will now tip the glass upside down over Mum's head but the water will stay in the glass."

"Er, do your trick over Desmond's head, please," said Mum.

"Over my head! No, thank you," Desmond said quickly.

"This trick will work, Desmond. I promise," Betsey pleaded.

"Oh, all right then," Desmond grumbled. "But I'd better not get wet, Betsey."

Betsey carefully put the piece of card on top of the full glass and then turned them both upside down. She then stretched out her arms until the glass was directly over Desmond's head.

"I don't like this . . ." Desmond said, hardly daring to blink.

"I will now take the card away and the water will stay in the glass," announced Betsey confidently.

"Betsey . . ."

"Trust me, Desmond," Betsey whispered.

Slowly, she removed the card. To everyone's amazement the water stayed in the glass. Mum, Gran'ma Liz and Sherena all started clapping, really impressed. Betsey grinned.

"It's working?" Desmond couldn't believe it. He looked up and WHOOSH! Water came flooding out all over his face.

Gran'ma Liz, Sherena and Mum all sprang off the sofa before they got drenched as well.

"Elizabeth Ruby Biggalow, just look what you've done to the sofa," Mum said.

"The clingfilm came off the top of the glass," Betsey wailed. "It wasn't meant to do that!"

Desmond leapt up, coughing and spluttering. "Look what you've done! I'm soaking wet!"

Mum, Sherena and Gran'ma Liz looked at him, flapping about like a fish out of water. They couldn't help it. They all burst out laughing!

"It's not funny," Desmond said, annoyed.

"Yes, it is!" Sherena grinned.

"Betsey, that's the first and last time I ever let you do your magic tricks anywhere near me," said Desmond crossly.

"But I've got a string trick, and a coin trick, and a marble trick to do yet," said Betsey.

"Betsey dear, I think it's time for you to call it a day," said Gran'ma Liz.

Gran'ma Liz went into the kitchen to get a drink, followed by Mum and Sherena. Desmond went to his bedroom to change his clothes, giving Betsey a dirty look on his way out of the living room.

Betsey sadly wandered out into the

front yard. Everything had gone wrong, wrong, wrong. Then Betsey spotted someone walking up the road who had her jumping up and down and gasping with excitement. She ran forward to meet him.

Five minutes later, Betsey ran into the house.

"Everyone! Everyone, where are you?" Betsey shouted.

Gran'ma Liz, Mum, Sherena and Desmond all came running.

"What's the matter, Betsey?"

"What's happened?"

"I've got another trick for you," said Betsey.

"Is that all?" Sherena frowned.

"Betsey, don't shout like that. I thought there was something wrong with you," said Mum.

"Please! Just one more trick. It's my best trick ever and this time it *will* work. Guaranteed!" said Betsey, excitedly.

"All right then. But this is the last one," said Mum.

"You've all got to stand over there," said Betsey. And she shooed her family over to the window.

Betsey walked back to the open living room door and stood by it.

"And now, Betsey the Tremendous, Betsey the Stupendous will make a real, live person appear before your very eyes," said Betsey proudly. "I'll just say the magic words first . . ."

"Oh, not again," said Sherena.

"I have to, or the trick won't work," said Betsey. Then she began. "Betsey Magic! Magic Betsey! Do your magic! Show us! Let's see!"

Betsey waved her wand three times in the air and – PEOUFF!

Dad sprang up from behind the sofa. "Hi there!" He grinned.

"DAD!"

The whole family came running over.

"I told you I was magic!" said Betsey proudly.

"You saw Dad outside and got him to sneak behind the sofa for your trick, didn't you?" asked Desmond.

"No, she didn't," said Dad, hugging everyone at once. "Betsey waved her wand and here I am! She really is Magic Betsey!"

And with that Dad winked at Betsey – and Betsey winked back!

Have you read these Betsey Biggalow books?

Have you read these Girl Wonder books?

Magic Betsey's Magnificent Wordsearch

There are ten words hidden in this wordsearch. Can you find them all?

U V Q H C P Y S S J Z Z
O U S A X E V T S B F V
L X R S S C D R A U R P
F D G T I P C I L G H Z
L G E G R Z P N G C P S
W B A T S E S G D N A D
P M N I O C T Z U W N O
W Z E V X O E A V O G D
J G R T T M P E W H U O
I H N E Y J E Y N S E D
S P W T M X P Y W A V Z
J T T R I C K Q U H J R

1. BETSEY
2. CARDS
3. COIN
4. GLASS
5. MAGIC
6. SHOW
7. STRING
8. TRICK
9. WAND
10. WATER

Turn to the back of the book to see the answers!

Spot the Difference

There are five differences between these two pictures. Can you spot them all?

Turn to the back of the book to see the answers!

Mind-blowing Magic Facts

- Magic tricks have amazed audiences for hundreds of years. The first ever book of magic tricks appeared in 1584.

- Erik Weisz was born in Budapest in 1874. He would grow up to become the most famous magician of all time, Harry Houdini.

- Harry Houdini was most famous for the art of *escapology* – the ability to escape from any trap, even when chained up! Don't attempt any of his tricks yourself though – a lot of them were very dangerous!

* There are magic societies all over the world which promote the art of stage magic. The most famous, The Magic Circle, was set up in London in 1905.

* One of the most well-known members of The Magic Circle is Prince Charles! He was accepted into the society in 1975 when he performed a classic "cup and balls" trick. He managed to make three small balls appear and disappear underneath three cups!

ANSWERS

Magic Betsey's Magnificent Wordsearch:

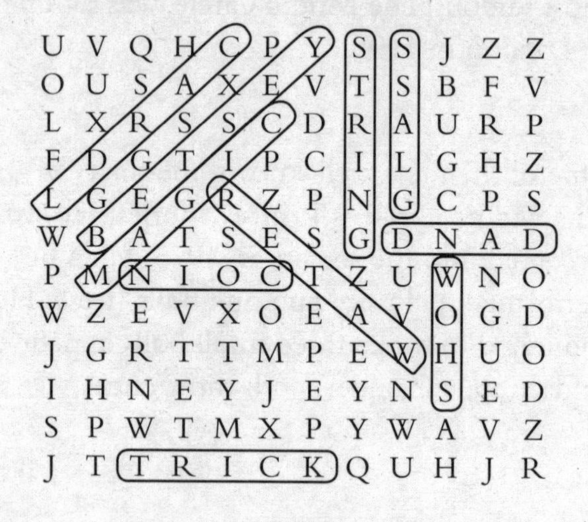

Spot the Difference: